Kookabu
Dreaming

Kookaburra Dreaming

Herbie Brennan

SCHOLASTIC
PRESS

Scholastic Children's Books,
Commonwealth House, 1–19 New Oxford Street,
London WC1A 1NU, UK
a division of Scholastic Ltd
London ~ New York ~ Toronto ~ Sydney ~ Auckland

First published by Scholastic Ltd, 1997

Copyright © Herbie Brennan, 1997

ISBN 0 590 54299 0

Typeset by DP Photosetting, Aylesbury, Bucks

Printed by Cox & Wyman Ltd, Reading, Berks

10 9 8 7 6 5 4 3 2 1

To Jacks, my inspiration,
with much love.

Chapter One

"Can anybody tell me what this is?" Mr Benson asked. He was holding up a long, battered, wooden tube.

There was silence in the class.

"This," said Mr Benson smugly, "is a didgeridoo." He smiled so that his teeth flashed through his brand-new tan. "Can anybody tell me what a didgeridoo might be?"

There was silence in the class.

Mr Benson's smile faded. "It's a musical instrument," he said. "Can anybody tell me who plays it?"

1

There was silence in the class.

Mr Benson's smile disappeared altogether. "Aborigines play it," he snapped. "Can anybody tell me where Aborigines come from?"

"Australia," Emma Preston told him promptly. Mr Benson had just returned from an Australian holiday, so it was a fair bet.

"Correct," said Mr Benson without much warmth. He could never understand why his pupils were so *slow*. "Can anybody tell me what's special about this particular didgeridoo?" He waved the instrument about so wildly that Thomas King, sitting in the front row, ducked.

There was silence in the class.

"What's special about this particular didgeridoo," said Mr Benson patiently, "is that it's the Sacred Didgeridoo of the Aranda Tribe – the only one of its kind in the whole world." His smile returned and his chest

2

puffed up like a pouter pigeon. "And I have brought it back with me!"

There was silence in the class, then Emma said, "They gave it to you?" She couldn't imagine why.

"Of course they didn't give it to me!" Mr Benson snapped. "I found it hidden in one of their caves. They're very stupid people, the Aranda Tribe. They believe ancestral ghosts will protect their property, so they don't even lock things up."

"You mean you sto— You mean you just took it?" Emma asked, appalled.

"Of course I took it," Mr Benson said impatiently. "I plan to donate it to the first museum that agrees to put my name prominently on the exhibit. And covers my expenses, of course."

"But what about the Aranda people?" Emma exclaimed. She could hardly believe what she was hearing, even from a pompous twit like her teacher.

"The didgeridoo will be much safer here in a museum. This artefact belongs to the whole world, not just a group of smelly natives who can't think of anything better to do than hide it away in a cave."

"But it's *theirs*!" Emma protested. "They *made* it."

Mr Benson opened the cupboard behind his desk and put the didgeridoo inside among the chalks and jotters needed to stuff his pupils' heads full of knowledge. "That may be so," he said, "but they obviously don't know how to look after it." He sniffed. "Leaving it guarded by a ghost, indeed!"

"But, Mr Benson – " Emma stopped abruptly. Through the classroom window she had suddenly caught sight of a terrifying dead-white face glaring malevolently at the teacher.

Chapter Two

Cheekyfella Tabagee had a Kookaburra Dreaming. It came about this way:

When Cheekyfella was a little thing curled up sleeping in his mother's womb, not yet alive, but certainly not dead, his mother went walkabout.

She walked by the billabong. She walked by the gum trees. She walked along the ridge of hills that stretched across the sandy desert to the far horizon.

And as she walked, it happened she walked upon a song line that was laid down by the

Ancestors long, long ago in the days of the Dreamtime. As the Ancestors moved about the land, they sang and left a trail of music. Along these song lines they scattered spirit children who scuttled down to lurk beneath the ground.

And wait.

As Cheekyfella's mother walked upon the song line, a spirit child jumped up and climbed on to her toenail. Then it crawled along her leg and swam into her womb. There it sang softly to Cheekyfella until he woke up. First thing Cheekyfella did when he woke up was kick.

Cheekyfella's mother felt the kick and knew the child inside her now had spirit life. So she looked around to find which Ancestor had sung the song line.

On her right was a rock of the Kookaburra Man. On her left was a bush of the Kookaburra Man. Behind her was an outcrop of sandstone sung up by the

Kookaburra Man. Before her was a stand of bush-oak sung up by the Kookaburra Man.

So Cheekyfella's mother knew that Cheekyfella had two fathers now – her husband Joe Tabagee who helped her make Cheekyfella's little body, and the Kookaburra Man, who gave her Cheekyfella's soul.

So when Cheekyfella came to be born, he was born into the Kookaburra Clan. The Kookaburra bird was his brother. He could no more hunt it for food than he could eat his own sister. Cheekyfella had a Kookaburra Dreaming.

Cheekyfella's father Joe had a Yellow Dog Dingo Dreaming. His mother had a Wallaby Dreaming. He had cousins with an Akuka Dreaming, friends with an Old Man Kangaroo Dreaming.

But as Cheekyfella soon discovered, he was the only member of the whole Aranda People at that time who had a Kookaburra Dreaming.

Chapter Three

One day, a white man drove into Aranda territory and set up survey gear.

He was spotted by a youngster who was called Spider Thompson on account of the way he skittered round the place and had a habit of hiding under rocks. Spider watched for a while from a gully, then slipped off to tell the Aranda headman Wally Arkady.

Wally brought a small party with him to see what was up. They fanned out and approached the white man much the same way they would creep up on a big boomer in a hunt.

The white man never saw them. He set his theodolite and made his measurements and after a while packed the whole lot into the back of his Jeep and went home.

Wally and the boys reckoned he was up to no good and it turned out they were right.

No more than a month after the surveyor came, a whole team of white men turned up at the spot he'd been measuring. Only they came with big yellow dozers, JCBs and drilling rigs instead of survey gear.

This time Wally and the boys didn't creep up quietly. The boys trotted in directly and sat down in front of the machines while Wally chatted with the foreman.

Turned out to be real bad news. The surveyor fella had discovered there were minerals underneath whole big sweeps of the Aranda homeland. The crew with the yellow dozers had come to dig them out.

"So you'd better tell your boys to move so

I can get on with my job," the foreman said to Wally Arkady.

But Wally didn't tell the boys to move. Instead he trotted off to talk to Mr Brownlow, who was the local Commissioner for Aboriginal Affairs.

"It's our land, Harry," he said firmly.

But Harry Brownlow put on a pained expression. "Now, Wally, we can't be absolutely sure of that," he said.

At this stage the Aranda People had lived in Aranda Territory for maybe forty thousand years. But that didn't count for much unless you had a bit of paper that *proved* the land was yours.

"You know we got that bit of paper," Wally said. "Our people signed it back in 1866." He was talking about a Treaty with the British giving the Aranda title to their land in return for a promise to stop stealing British sheep.

"*You* know that and *I* know that," Harry

Brownlow said placatingly, "but the question now is: where to *find* that bit of paper."

Wally's brown eyes narrowed. "Find it in Melbourne, Harry. That's where your Government keeps all the old papers."

At which point Harry Brownlow had the good grace to look embarrassed. "Well, now, that's the problem, Wally. Seems that old treaty has got itself mislaid. The boys from the mining company are claiming the land's up for grabs."

They batted the whole thing back and forward for a while. Wally got angry and stubborn by turns, but none of it made much difference. The one thing he had going for him was that his boys were squatting in front of the machines and wouldn't move until he told them.

Eventually Harry Brownlow said, "Tell you what I'll do, Wally. You get your boys to move and I'll make an order stopping the mining company from doing anything until we have a real good search for that old treaty. Must be a copy somewhere. If there is, I'm sure we'll turn it up."

"And if there isn't?" Wally asked.

A pained look took hold of Harry Brownlow's features. "Then we'll have to let the mining company go ahead. Can't stand in the way of progress."

Chapter Four

Harry Brownlow wasn't a bad stick for a white man. At least he kept his word. The people from the mining company pulled out next day. But Wally noticed they left their rigs behind. Once the Government in Melbourne decided they couldn't find a copy of the treaty, the miners could be back and ripping up the land in hours.

Wally took the crisis to the Council of Aranda Elders and the Aranda Elders decided it was time to sing the ancient songs that stopped the land returning to the way it used to be, way back in the Dreamtime.

In the Dreamtime when the world was young, the Earth was just a murky plain washed by a grey salt sea and covered by a twilight sky. On its surface there was nothing except a few hollows that would one day become waterholes.

But underneath the surface of the earth was the sun and the moon and the stars and animals and plants all waiting to be born. Underneath each hollow lay an Ancestor.

On the morning of the First Day, the sun was born. It burst through the surface and flooded the land with golden light. Its rays warmed the hollows where the Ancestors lay dozing.

The heat awoke them and one by one these sleeping greybeards pushed their bodies through the mud and cracked their eyelids open. Out they came, one after one: the Carpet Snake Man, the Witchetty Grub Man, the Cockatoo Man, the Honey-Ant, the Bandicoot, Old Man Kangaroo, Mister

Platypus, and many more.

Each one put his left foot forward and began to sing the land into existence.

Each one walked the great old paths, singing up the rocks and waterholes, the eucalyptus trees, the rivers and the ranges, the salt pans, spinifex and sand dunes, the reed beds and the gum trees.

But the land wouldn't stay that way unless the Aranda repeated the old Singing.

This meant they had to call all the Aranda People together for a Singing. Every man and every woman of the People had their own song linked to a special place. When the songs were sung in the right order, they held the land firm until the next Singing.

There had been regular Singings to hold the land firm right back to the Dreamtime when the Ancestors sung it up in the first place. But this was going to be the most important Singing of all. Because this Singing was the one that would hold the land for the Aranda People. This Singing would make sure the mining company didn't get its way.

Everybody came to a Singing. Everybody knew the order of his song, because to sing a song out of its place would start an earthquake.

Since olden times, the Singing had been held at a place called Middle Bone, a flatland far out in the bush between Twin Hills and the dried-up bed of Caterpillar Creek. There was a cave in one of the Twin Hills where the People kept the sacred instruments they needed for the Singing – the sacred click-sticks and the sacred didgeridoo.

When the Elders decided on a special Singing, a Clever Man of the Aranda put the word out on the wind. As the wind blew here and there, from one end of Australia to the other, all the far-flung members of the Aranda People heard the call.

Among them were Joe Tabagee and his

young son Cheekyfella, who was at that time ten years old.

Joe Tabagee worked for the white man in a saw mill. Cheekyfella worked there too, after a fashion. The white man's law didn't allow anybody to employ children under fifteen, but Cheekyfella sometimes ran errands for the men at the mill and cleaned up a bit at the end of the day and the white man gave him a few cents here, a few cents there.

The mill was south of Alice, which was quite a way away from Middle Bone. All the same, the call came to them loud and clear.

"Hear that, Cheekyfella?" Joe asked, sniffing the air with his broad, flat nose.

"For sure, Da," Cheekyfella told him, even though he hadn't actually heard the call like he was hearing his father now. It was more as if the wind had got into his ear and carried the Clever Man's words into his head so that he heard them in his mind.

So Joe Tabagee and Cheekyfella stopped

what they were doing, took off all their clothes and walked out of the lumber yard.

At the same time, all over the land in the builder's yards and the sheep farms and the factory sheds, Aranda people stopped what they were doing, stepped out of their clothes and went walkabout into the bush.

Their employers were none too pleased, of course, but there was nothing they could do. There was no following the Aranda. White men got lost in the bush. The Aranda had their secret ways.

So one by one or in little groups, the Aranda found their way to Middle Bone. Joe and Cheekyfella were among the last to arrive, part because they had so far to walk, part because Joe turned aside to visit the grave of Cheekyfella's mother who had died two summers earlier.

When they did get to Middle Bone, Joe and Cheekyfella saw a great gathering of the Aranda People spread across the flatland, clumped in small groups, grinning, talking, joking, sharing food.

Some of the men carried spears and woomeras, more still carried boomerangs. Most of the women had bush-tucker bags around their waists for collecting grubs or roots or any other food they could find.

There were no houses, no huts, no humpies, no thorn shelters. Nobody wore clothes. The skin of the Aranda was a dusty black that did not burn in the sun.

"Wey-hey!" Joe Tabagee exclaimed, delighted. "See all the friends we're going to meet!"

Cheekyfella was pleased too. It had been a while.

As Joe and Cheekyfella started across the flatland to meet their friends, they noticed a cloud of dust rise up on the horizon. They stopped to watch. Soon others stopped to watch as well.

The cloud of dust came closer, covering a

noise like a great beast growling. Pretty soon everyone in the whole of Middle Bone was stopped and watching. Then the dust and noise resolved itself into a battered grey Land Cruiser that bounced and rattled along the parched bed of Caterpillar Creek.

The driver was a white man.

Chapter Five

The Land Cruiser left the creek bed and roared across the plain, scattering groups of the Aranda People. It careered up to Porcupine Rock where the tribal Elders were squatted in a sullen semi-circle. Brakes squealed, pebbles flew and the Land Cruiser stopped.

The driver leaped out. He was a tall man, thin as a stick insect, wearing khaki shorts, white shirt, white socks, brown boots and a bush hat dangling corks. Everything looked brand new, although the shirt was soaked in sweat.

"Good morning!" he said stridently. "Which of you speaks English?"

The Aranda headman, Wally Arkady, leaned over so his mouth was close to the ear of the Elder beside him. "Whinging Pom," he whispered.

The Elders stared at the stranger gloomily. None of them spoke or made to stand up.

"Come on now," the Englishman said encouragingly, "there must be at least one of you who understands what I'm saying!"

Elder Billy Nakamurra looked up at him and smiled benignly. "You have a face like a witchetty grub's backside," he said in the old Aranda tongue. "And you smell worse than a boomer's armpit."

There was a burst of laughter from his fellow Elders.

"No, no," said the Englishman, raising his voice as if everybody had gone deaf. "English. English." In his agitation he lapsed into pidgin. "You fella blackfellas come speak lingo like boss woman Queen fly back home cross big water." He dived one hand through the air and made a noise like an aeroplane.

"Ah, English!" Wally Arkady nodded sagely.

"Yes, yes," the Pom confirmed, excited and delighted. "Are you the boss man here?"

Wally looked up at the cloudless sky and pondered the question. He looked down at his callused feet and pondered it some more. Eventually he said, "Reckon."

The Pom stuck out his hand. "Arnold Benson. On holiday from Dorset, England. Pleased to meet you."

Wally wasn't known for his fondness of the white man and at any other time he might have stretched the game out a little. But he had a Singing to get underway. He climbed slowly to his feet and shook the outstretched hand. "Wally Arkady," he said. "Aranda headman."

"Mr Arkady," asked Arnold Benson, "are you people holding a Corroboree?"

Corroboree was what the white man called a Singing (or any other meeting of the People) because the People had taken great care never to tell the white man the real name.

"Maybe," said Wally Arkady suspiciously.

"What luck!" Mr Benson exclaimed. "This will make my holiday. I must get my camera!" He raced back to the Land Cruiser and stuck his head inside.

"This clown's fixing to stay," said Billy Nakamurra quietly.

"We have to get rid of him," said Timmy Stiga, another of the Elders. It was forbidden for a white man to witness a Singing.

"How we going to do that?" asked Billy.

"Same as always," Wally Arkady told him; and grinned.

Chapter Six

M r Benson emerged from the Land Cruiser with a Nikon round his neck and a camcorder in his hand. He beamed at anyone prepared to meet his eye.

"I am a schoolteacher," he announced. "Form master at St Cuthbert's, Bedchester." Then, when nobody paid attention, he pointed to his chest and shouted, "This fella here be a master man, knock clever stuff into thick heads stupid white kids." He waved his cameras. "This fella take pictures of you blackfellas show all chillun back home."

"Try the old lost soul trick," Timmy Stiga advised quietly in Aranda.

"No pictures!" Wally called at once in English. "White man's picture box will steal our souls." Somehow he managed to keep from smiling.

"Nonsense!" Mr Benson snapped. "Rank superstition. Your souls are quite safe – you have my personal guarantee of that."

Wally looked at Timmy who shrugged slightly. "Worth a try," he said in Aranda.

"Everybody happy with Plan B?" Wally asked, also in Aranda.

The Elders wrinkled their flat noses, scowled a little at Mr Benson, then one by one nodded. They climbed to their feet and moved out among the People, quietly chanting in Aranda, "Plan B ... Plan B ... Plan B..."

Wally grinned. "Let the Corroboree begin!" he called in English.

At once the nearest group began line

dancing. Beyond them, an old greybeard named Wallaby Sam started to show off the hand jive he'd learned at the Mission back in the Sixties. Timmy Stiga bent one knee and stamped the foot vigorously to lead off an old fashioned square dance. Billy Nakamurra, who liked country and western, let rip with a tuneless version of *Stand by Your Man,* carefully translating the words into Aranda.

"Come on," grinned Joe Tabagee at Cheekyfella. He started disco dancing.

Cheekyfella, who knew Plan B as well as any of them, grinned back at his dad and did a moonwalk fit to knock out Michael Jackson.

In a minute it had spread right across the gathering at Middle Bone. The Aranda People leaped and twisted, ducked and dived, sang and shouted, jumped and squatted, bopped, hopped, spun and did break dancing. Mr Arnold ran amongst them, camcorder whirring, Nikon clicking, convinced he was recording a genuine Aboriginal Corroboree.

"Rock 'n' roll!" Wally Arkady exclaimed.

The Aranda People kept this nonsense up for close on half an hour, then, when Mr Benson showed no sign of tiring, Tilly Popanji, a fat girl with boundless energy, grabbed him and whirled him round until he staggered dizzily away.

"I think perhaps I'll drive back to town and have a little lie down," he muttered to no one in particular. He walked, swaying, to the Land Cruiser, sat in it for a while to settle down, then drove off slowly back along the bed of Caterpillar Creek.

"Right on, Tilly!" Wally called.

The Aranda People stopped leaping round like lunatics and watched Mr Benson leave. Plan B had worked again. They watched as the Land Cruiser left the creek bed and headed out towards Twin Hills where, to their surprise, it stopped. Mr Benson got out, and disappeared among some rocks near the sacred cave.

"Probably had a call of nature after all that dancing," Timmy Stiga grinned.

Which seemed to be the truth of it because he hurried back to the Land Cruiser only minutes later. Billy Nakamurra, who had a Hawk Dreaming, said he thought the white fella was carrying something, but even Billy's eyesight couldn't make out what at that distance.

Chapter Seven

When the Land Cruiser eventually disappeared over the horizon, the Aranda People squatted or lay down to rest a while from their exertions.

"How come the white folks keep bothering us?" Cheekyfella Tabagee asked his father Joe. Cheekyfella hadn't much experience of white folks outside the saw mill and no experience at all of white folks all the way from England. But he knew white folks often turned up uninvited when the People held a gathering. That's why everybody learned Plan B.

"The white folks think that what we do is cute," his father said. "They don't understand how important it is for the land."

"So they come to take pictures?"

His father nodded. "And get in the way."

"How come Wally doesn't tell them it's important?" Cheekyfella asked. Everybody in the tribe knew Wally was real smart despite the way he looked. Cheekyfella sort of assumed the white folks would respect him too.

But Joe Tabagee sighed. "Son," he said, "our people have been trying to talk sense into the white folks ever since they found Australia. That was back in 1642 and we haven't made an inch of headway yet."

Just then Wally Arkady gave a signal. Joe and Cheekyfella left off talking and walked to join in the preparations for the real Singing.

Scattered groups of the Aranda People drifted slowly together to form a black lake in the middle of the plain, then split into two long, straggling columns like gigantic ants. The women made up one column, the men the other.

The two columns shifted and drifted until they ran parallel to one another, a man facing a woman, a woman facing a man, more or less. Everybody took part except for Wally and a handful of the Elders, who climbed on top of Porcupine Rock to oversee proceedings.

"Start the dance!" called Wally.

The People were now so strung out his voice would not carry far enough, but those nearest him took up the order and passed it on so that it reached the farthest ends of the two lines way beyond the old stream bed of Caterpillar Creek.

The lines began to move, slowly at first but with gathering speed. At first the movement was jerky. Each member of a line would stamp a foot then take a step. *Stamp, step, jerk forward* went the line. But after a minute or so they got the rhythm so the movement became fluid.

STAMP! together went the feet and the sound echoed like a giant thud across the bush. *Shuffle* went each line, then *STAMP* again then *shuffle forward.*

Without having to be told, the People slapped their thighs at every step. *STAMP ... SLAP ... FORWARD ... STAMP ... SLAP ... FORWARD...* Then the lines began to weave into one another like two snakes curling round a rod. *STAMP ... SLAP ... FORWARD ... WEAVE...*

After a while of this, one of the women began to sing. Her voice was high and clear and carried like a swooping bird across the plain.

Chapter Eight

Up on Porcupine Rock, Wally felt a lump in his throat. This was the time he got so proud of his People he felt like he might burst.

A man caught up the song, backing it with rhythm, a growling grunt in a language that was older even than Aranda – as old, some said, as the Ancestors themselves.

STAMP ... SLAP ... SHUFFLE ... WEAVE ... SOARING BIRDSONG ... GRUNTING RHYTHM...

Another moment and the one man's rough grunt had been joined by another and another until it became a low, growling chant that caught the soul and shook it sideways.

Another woman sang, taking verses from the first. Another carried these songs forward, then another and another in her turn. Then two women sang together, then three, then a whole choir.

All the while the two lines of moving dancers twined in and out around each other in a spiral snake across the plain.

Watching, Wally Arkady felt the old deep satisfaction. Despite the interruption of the stupid white man, it was going well. He turned to Timmy Stiga who crouched beside him. "Bring the click-sticks and the didgi, Timmy."

"Right, Wally," Timmy nodded. He jumped down off the rock and set off at a trot across the plain.

The rhythm deepened. The song swooped and soared. Verse followed verse as men and women began to change about, women taking up the rhythm, men taking up the verse. The Aranda People had started to sing up the land.

The two lines split again and swung out like a fountain, then formed a massive spinning circle that moved in time to the rhythm of the stamping feet.

The First Singing was coming to an end.

The circle spun. The singing slowed and slowed, then dropped into a heady chant. The People were calling on the Spirit Child, the first human being the Ancestors made all that time ago in the Dreaming.

Down on the plain, young Cheekyfella joined the chant, holding his father's hand. Up on Porcupine Rock, Wally Arkady grinned from pure joy.

As if in answer to the call, out of the circle shuffled a thin, grey-bearded man. Josh Goolagong was by far the oldest of the People, so ancient folks used to joke he half-remembered the Ancestors themselves. But he was a fit old buzzard and did a little dance step just to show off before he squatted in the centre of the circle, waiting.

Old Josh Goolagong was waiting to make special music. He was waiting for the sacred didgeridoo. With it, he would lead the Singing that would make the ceremony complete and safeguard the land.

The circle spun. The chant became faster and faster, more and more excited. Out of the corner of his eye, Wally spotted Timmy Stiga bounding like a frightened boomer across the plain.

Timmy's job now was to slip through the moving circle and hand the didgeridoo to Josh. He would play the sacred clicksticks himself. Together Tim and Josh would lead the People in the final magic song. When it was done, the land was safe.

But Timmy didn't slip through the moving circle. In fact, he didn't go near the circle at all. Instead he kept on coming until he reached Porcupine Rock.

"What's wrong, Tim?" Wally asked, his eyes still on the waiting Josh.

"I got the clicksticks, Wally," Timmy told him breathlessly, "but somebody has made off with the didgeridoo!"

Chapter Nine

"What's happening, Pa?" asked Cheekyfella Tabagee, looking round him with wide eyes. The singing had stopped, the dancing had stopped, the chanting had stopped and there was a big panic on for sure.

"The Pom in the Land Cruiser stole our didgeridoo," Joe Tabagee told him sourly. "Means we can't finish out the Singing."

Cheekyfella frowned. Lots of the Aranda had a didgi, including his father. "Why don't you lend them yours?" he asked.

"Not as simple as that, son," Joe told him.

"What the Pom took was our *sacred* didgeridoo. Made right back in the Dreamtime so they say. Ordinary didgi won't do, you see. Has to be that one, otherwise we can't finish off the Singing."

Cheekyfella's frown deepened. "What happens if we can't finish off the Singing, Pa?"

Joe Tabagee looked bleak. "Well, what we done so far will hold things for a few weeks or a month, maybe. But if we don't finish the Singing, the land will fall apart."

Cheekyfella blinked. "All of it?"

"Yeah."

"All of *Australia*?" Cheekyfella asked, appalled.

"Singing's the only thing that's held it together all these years," his father said. "That's what the white man never figured." He sighed. "This year we got a little trouble from the mining company as well."

They were drifting, along with the rest of the gathering, towards Porcupine Rock where Wally and the Elders were confabing with the Clever Men.

"So what are we going to do, boys?" Wally asked the Clever Men worriedly.

A Clever Man called Scratching Woman stared out towards the Twin Hills, scowling hugely. "Got to send somebody after the Pom, Wally. Got to get our didgi back."

"I know that, Scratch," Wally said impatiently. "What I want you boys to tell me is who should go. Wallaby Sam's the best tracker we have, but he's forgetful. Timmy's next best, but I can't spare him. Besides, not everybody's allowed to handle the sacred didgi. We got enough trouble already without offending the ghost."

Scratching Woman and the other clever men huddled. After a while they broke up and Scratching Woman said to Wally, "Got to ask the spirits, Wally."

"Well, why don't you do just that?" Wally suggested.

The tribespeople who had been drifting towards the rock, stopped and watched warily. Asking spirits anything was a heavy number, even for a Clever Man and nobody wanted to get too close. At the same time, nobody wanted to miss anything either.

The Clever Men went back into a huddle. This time when they broke up, one of their number squatted down to build a little fire. He used bits of the dried up bush that grew all over Middle Bone, setting it together in a special way. Then he rubbed two sticks together to make a spark. After a while, Wally handed him a disposable lighter and the fire suddenly flared into life.

When the tinder was well caught, Scratching Woman sprinkled on some dried herbs that sent up clouds of stifling smoke.

"Gee, Scratch, do you have to do that?" Wally asked, coughing.

"Got to, Wally," Scratch confirmed. "Smoke's what calls the spirits."

Wally backed off a pace or two. But Scratching Woman and the other Clever Men huddled round the fire and breathed the smoke.

"What are they doing, Pa?" frowned Cheekyfella.

"They're getting set to travel to the Spirit Land," Joe Tabagee told him.

Cheekyfella watched carefully. Despite what his father said, the Clever Men didn't seem to be going anywhere. But they all looked peculiar. Their eyes were rolling upwards and their bodies were trembling like leaves in the wind. Cheekyfella expected it came from breathing too much smoke. Suddenly they all fell down.

"Are they dead?" asked Cheekyfella curiously.

"Nah!" Joe Tabagee shook his head. "They just flew off to Spirit Land."

Scratching Woman sat up again, then stood, all in a single impossible movement.

He looked dreadful. His eyes were wide open, blank and staring. His mouth was twisted and drooling. There were lines on his face that hadn't been there before and his colour was so pale he was starting to look like a Pom.

"What's the matter with Scratch, Pa?" Cheekyfella asked.

"Spirit's got him," Joe explained. "It'll talk to us in a minute."

Scratching Woman's mouth opened and a huge voice emerged. The words were so loud they carried right across the Middle Bone.

"YOU MUST SEND THE ONE WITH THE SPECIAL DREAMING TO BRING BACK THE SACRED DIDGERIDOO!" the spirit voice boomed.

"Who's the one with the special dreaming, Spirit?" asked Wally Arkady.

Scratching Woman's body rotated slowly and one arm came up with a pointing finger. "THAT ONE, WALLY!" boomed the spirit. "HE HAS A KOOKABURRA DREAMING!"

Cheekyfella suddenly felt cold. The finger was pointing straight at him.

Chapter Ten

One of the women gave Cheekyfella a tucker-bag with a few witchetties for the journey. Wally Arkady gave him a spear taller than himself. His pa gave him three boomerangs.

"Why three, Pa?" Cheekyfella asked.

"One to hunt. One to sell going. One to sell coming back," Joe said. "White fellas pay a good price for a real boomerang. Can't seem to get the hang of making decent ones themselves."

"Yanks pay the most," Timmy Stiga put in helpfully. "They're the ones with palm trees on their shirts."

"Thanks, Timmy," Cheekyfella said. He was excited by the prospect of the journey and a little fearful. But most of all, he was enjoying the attention.

Scratching Woman handed him something wrapped in platy-skin. "Reckon you'll need these for when you find the didgi," he said soberly.

"What are they, Scratch?" asked Cheekyfella, peering inside.

"Paints," said Scratching Woman. "I know the spirit picked you, but it's still bad luck to handle the sacred didgi unless you paint your face white first."

Billy Nakamurra shouldered his way to the front. "Does that mean the teacher fella got himself a wodge of bad luck, Scratch?" he asked.

Scratching Woman frowned. "Not sure, Billy. That fella's got a white face to begin with."

"But Cheekyfella will be all right if he paints his face?" Billy persisted.

"For sure," said Scratching Woman. The group around them nodded sagely in approval.

"You know what you have to do, son?" Joe Tabagee asked anxiously.

It was simple enough, but very difficult. Cheekyfella was supposed to pick up Schoolteacher Benson's trail and follow it wherever it went. Since Schoolteacher Benson was driving a Land Cruiser, everybody reckoned it could take a while before Cheekyfella managed to catch up with him, unless the thing broke down.

So Cheekyfella had been instructed to keep going even if the trail led out of the bush and into white man territory. Things could get a lot more tricky there, but the sacred didgeridoo was too important to start worrying about problems.

Sooner or later, everybody said,

Cheekyfella was bound to catch up with Schoolteacher Benson. When he did, he was to hang around until the opportunity arose, then *take the didgi back*! But he had to be careful, especially if he was in white man territory. He couldn't just grab the didgi, otherwise Schoolteacher Benson could have him for assault. He had to take it stealthily.

And when he took it stealthily, he had to make sure he wasn't caught. Even though the sacred didgi had belonged to the Aranda People since the Dreamtime, everybody knew you couldn't trust the white folks when it came to fair play.

Cheekyfella nodded. He knew what he had to do all right.

"Well," said Joe Tabagee, "best be off while the trail's still fresh."

"Right, Pa," Cheekyfella said. He dropped the paints into his tucker-bag and wrapped the bag around with his shirt and shorts for when he left the bush. Then he tied the bundle to his spear, slung it over his shoulder, clasped the boomerangs in his other hand and trotted off.

"Bye, Cheekyfella," Wally called. "Come back with the didgi and we'll make your pa an Elder."

"Bye, Cheekyfella," called the Elders.

"Bye, Cheekyfella," called the women and his friends.

"Bye, son. Send us a card," called his father.

But Cheekyfella scarcely heard them. His eyes were fixed on the tracks of the Land Cruiser that crawled along the length of Caterpillar Creek.

Chapter Eleven

It got more tricky as he went along.

Once the Land Cruiser left Caterpillar Creek, it had moved on to rocky ground where no tracks showed. All Cheekyfella had to go on was the odd broken bush, the occasional squashed bug. The signs were there all right, but they took a lot of patience to find.

After a while, he decided to try figuring in place of tracking. Middle Bone wasn't exactly close to any towns, but the closest two were Harrison Ridge due south and Little Blue to the south east. Harrison

Ridge was the larger of the two and got a lot of tourists in the summer. Cheekyfella figured Schoolteacher Benson likely came from there, so he headed south, looking for tracks.

It was a sensible enough guess, but it was wrong. After a while he had to admit to himself he'd made a mistake. He headed for Little Blue.

Little Blue was a miserable sort of town. It was built in 1900 on the promise of a gold rush, then stranded when the gold ran out in 1901. But it was a stubborn sort of town as well. It had struggled on in its own miserable way ever since.

Lately the misery had started to pay off. Little Blue had never been able to afford things like proper streets or new buildings.

The result was it still looked like a frontier town. A few tourists were coming to see that. Cheekyfella knew Schoolteacher Benson had to be one of them.

But the problem was exactly where to find him.

Cheekyfella stared gloomily at the unmade road into Little Blue. Out in the bush, tracking became a problem when signs were few. Here it was a problem because signs were just too many. There must have been a hundred vehicles on this bit of road in the last few days and all of them left tracks.

Winston Churchill Japurula was squatting by the roadside, wearing torn shorts and a dirty shirt. Winston Churchill was Pintupi, but a good friend of the Aranda. He hung around Little Blue a lot, bumming chocolate and doing odd jobs when he was desperate.

"Hey, Winston Churchill," Cheekyfella said, "you reckon these were made by a Land Cruiser?" He pointed to a particular set of tracks, more recent than the rest.

Winston Churchill scarcely glanced in his direction. "Nope," he said.

Cheekyfella frowned. "You sure, Winston Churchill?"

Winston Churchill stood up, came over and stared at the tracks. He sucked his bottom lip thoughtfully. "I reckon, Cheekyfella, them tracks were made by an open lorry with four passengers, one of them a woman, all of them white, carrying a load of machine parts and a five gallon drum of diesel fuel."

"Wow!" said Cheekyfella, impressed. "You can tell all that just by looking at the *tracks*?"

"Naw." Winston Churchill shook his head. "I just fell off the back of the blooming thing!"

"Any Poms in Little Blue just now?" Cheekyfella asked.

Winston Churchill shrugged. "Place is crawling with them."

"I'm tracking one called Schoolteacher Benson."

"Dopey-looking fella without much meat on him?"

"That's him," Cheekyfella nodded. "He stole our sacred didgi."

Winston Churchill went back to squatting by the side of the road. He fished a soggy chocolate bar from the pocket of his shirt, handed Cheekyfella a square and ate one himself. "Reckon you're in luck," he said. "That fella's staying in Mrs O'Malley's guest house."

But Cheekyfella wasn't in luck. When he got to Mrs O'Malley's Guest House he found Schoolteacher Benson had checked out no more than an hour before.

According to Mrs O'Malley, he was heading for the airport. Carrying a didgeridoo. And catching the next plane back to Pomland.

Chapter Twelve

Cheekyfella had never been to an airport before and he didn't like it. He didn't like the smells. He didn't like the noise. He didn't like the crowds. But he did like the planes.

"Hey, young fella, where do you think you're going?"

Cheekyfella turned towards the man in uniform. "Going to catch a plane to Pomland," he said politely.

"Not without a ticket you aren't," the man told him, kindly enough.

"How much is a ticket?" Cheekyfella asked.

He knew from working at the mill that everything was money with the white man.

"Oh," said the man casually, "about twelve hundred dollars." He grinned. "Unless you want to go first class."

"Is that less?" asked Cheekyfella hopefully.

"More," the man said firmly.

Cheekyfella trotted off, wondering how he could earn twelve hundred dollars in a hurry. He was sitting on a bench, still wondering, when he saw a familiar face.

Johnny Oodnadatta was Pintupi like Winston Churchill Japurula. Cheekyfella knew him because, like Cheekyfella, he had a Kookaburra Dreaming. He was pushing a trolley piled with buckets and a broom.

"G'day, Cheekyfella," he said cheerfully. "What brings you all the way out here?"

"Tracking a Pom, Johnny," said Cheekyfella gloomily, "only he's gone back to Pomland and I don't have twelve hundred dollars."

"Is this the Pom that stole your sacred didgi?" Johnny asked. "I heard about it on the grapevine."

Cheekyfella nodded.

"Can't let him away with that," said Johnny Oodnadatta. "You come with me, Cheek."

Cheekyfella followed Johnny Oodnadatta out of the terminal building, along a path and through a gate. A different man in uniform was leaning on a little hut, smoking a cigarette. "Who's the kid, Johnny?" he asked casually.

"Nephew," Johnny told him shortly. "Giving me a hand to load the 747."

The man waved them through.

Cheekyfella found himself on a runway beside a plane with *QANTAS* painted on the side. It looked like an enormous silver bird. Men were loading cargo into an open hold. None of them was an Aranda, but all of them were black.

"Hold on a minute," Johnny said. He strolled over to the group, had a few words then strolled back again. "All fixed up," he said casually. "I told them about the didgi."

The men packed Cheekyfella into a slatted wooden crate. There was no room for his spear, but he took the tucker-bag and boomerangs. Johnny dropped in a tattered woollen sweater. "Better take this, Cheek," he said. "You wouldn't believe how cold it gets in Pomland. Specially during summer."

They put the lid on the crate, but only knocked in two thin tacks. "One good push and you're out," Johnny told him through the slats. "You got tucker for the trip?"

"Sure thing, Johnny," Cheekyfella said. He still had most of his witchetties. A thought struck him. "Won't the fella at the gate think it's funny when you go back without me?"

"Naw," said Johnny carelessly. "White

folks never look at any of us properly. He won't even notice."

Cheekyfella squatted down in the crate.

"Good luck with the tracking, Cheek!" Johnny called. Then everything went dark as the men closed the door of the cargo hold. Cheekyfella waited.

After a while the plane shook, then began to move. A short time after that, Cheekyfella's stomach dropped down somewhere near his feet and he reckoned that he must be flying now.

Chapter Thirteen

Johnny Oodnadatta was dead right about the cold. Even with the sweater on, Cheekyfella Tabagee shivered in the British sunshine.

He'd sneaked out of the warehouse where his crate had been unloaded, thinking he would walk to Dorset once he found the right direction. Now he thought he'd better sell a boomerang and buy more clothes. He wandered off to find somebody with a palm tree on his shirt.

The airport was enormous, far bigger than the one he'd left in Australia. The noise and the crowds and the smell were even worse. Cheekyfella took one look and decided to put up with the cold for a while. He'd sell a boomerang later. Right now all he wanted was to get away to somewhere quiet.

Only problem was to find the exit.

Fifteen minutes later, Cheekyfella was still looking. Out in the bush he could find his way anywhere, but this airport was something else again. He wondered if he should ask directions.

A party of schoolchildren swarmed out of a doorway and surrounded him. They seemed to come in assorted colours and several different sizes. He picked a pretty dark girl.

"Excuse me," he said politely, "but can you tell me how to get out of here and point me on the way to Dorset?"

The girl smiled, but shook her head. "Je ne comprends pas anglais," she said.

Cheekyfella blinked. He turned to a boy with close-cropped blond hair. "Excuse—"

But the boy was already shaking his head as well. "Nein," he said helplessly.

"You – yes, you child! Get in line!"

Cheekyfella jumped. A middle-aged woman with a rolled umbrella was bearing down on him, a small dog trotting at her heels. She looked as terrifying as an eight foot perenty lizard.

"Come on!" the woman said. "Don't dawdle or we'll miss the coach!"

"Excuse—" Cheekyfella began a third time, then stopped. If this party was going for a coach, it meant they were leaving the airport. All he had to do was tag along and slip away once they all got outside.

"What is it?" snapped the woman crossly.

"Nothing," Cheekyfella said. He smiled at her.

The woman did not smile back. "Get in line!" she told him sternly, prodding him a little with the end of her umbrella. Cheekyfella got in line.

A black boy about his own age gave him a beaming smile. "Man, that Mrs Preston is one tough banana! Hey, where you from?" he asked in English.

"Oz," said Cheekyfella. "Where are you from?"

"Belize," said the black boy. "Isn't this great?" He stuck out his hand. "Thomas King."

Cheekyfella shook it. "Cheekyfella Tabagee," he said.

The party surged forward. The woman with the umbrella knew her way around because five minutes later they were all standing in a massive car park beside a sleek new coach with *INTERNATIONAL STUDENT EXCHANGE PROGRAMME* blazoned on the side.

"Well, so long, Thomas," Cheekyfella said. He made to slip away.

"Just where do you think you're going?" asked the woman with the umbrella. She glared at him. "There's a loo on the coach if you need one!"

But Cheekyfella didn't answer. He was already half-way across the car park, heading for the exit.

Chapter Fourteen

It was nothing like anything he'd seen in Australia. The airport seemed to go on forever and when he finally left it, the countryside was all a hideous green. Even in the sunshine, everything felt damp. He kept seeing streams and ponds, rivers and lakes. The whole country was so wet it was amazing nobody turned mouldy.

The only really good thing was the roads. Back home there were no roads at all in the bush, just beaten tracks and precious few of those. It was only in the white man's territory that you found roads worth talking about.

But here in Pomland, roads were everywhere. They ran north and south and east and west and all points in between. They circled the cities and linked even the most tiny villages. Cheekyfella figured Mr Spider must have sung up the tracks because they made a web across the entire country.

So many roads made finding your way very easy. Cheekyfella sold a boomerang to a loud, fat giant with a palm tree on his shirt and used some of the proceeds to buy a map. He was good with maps – a skill his father taught him – and found Dorset at once.

Finding Bedchester took a little longer, but not much. There seemed to be a hundred roads heading roughly in the right direction. Cheekyfella folded the map and dropped it in his tucker-bag, took a bearing from the sun and trotted off.

It took him all of thirty seconds to discover that the roads were dangerous. In the parts of Australia he knew well, you got the odd road train and a few Land Cruisers rattling down the big through-routes. Here in Pomland there were hundreds of cars and scores of trucks.

Worse still, the drivers all looked strung out. He saw one behind the wheel of a lorry who couldn't have looked more worried if he'd been sharing the cab with a croc. Cheekyfella took to the verge, then, when even that didn't feel too safe, climbed a fence and trotted onwards in a field, keeping the road in sight as a guide.

On the second day it rained.

Cheekyfella knew it must be rain because his father had once talked to him about water that fell from the sky while Cheekyfella was just a little kid. Cheekyfella didn't remember and only half believed it until Spider Thompson told him you could rely on rain maybe once in seven years around the area of Middle Bone – something he'd had from *his* father.

Now he could see it for himself, it wasn't at all what he'd expected. It was water from the sky all right, but it came down in drops, not sheets, and it went on and on.

Cheekyfella stood staring upwards into a sky that had turned from normal blue into something nearly black, hardly able to believe he was getting wet all over with water from the sky. He smiled and water dripped into his mouth. He laughed aloud and danced about in his excitement.

He felt quite disappointed when it stopped.

Nights got so cold he slept in barns when he could and burrowed into haystacks when he couldn't. The witchetty grubs had run out, but he was able to dig more roots than he could eat and hunted rabbit with his two remaining boomerangs. All in all, he did quite well for tucker.

After five days' steady travelling, he passed a big black and gold sign that said WELCOME TO DORSET. Two days later he was trotting into Bedchester.

Now all he had to do was find St Cuthbert's and Schoolteacher Benson.

Chapter Fifteen

Cheekyfella Tabagee squatted on the pavement watching the big gates of St Cuthbert's School the way his dad had taught him to watch a lizard's burrow when he was hunting. Beside him sat an old geezer with dark glasses and a white stick who had a tin cup in front of him on which he'd propped a notice saying:

> BLIND
> PLEASE HELP

It was still quite early and only a handful of

pupils had turned up so far, but already Cheekyfella noticed more black faces than he had expected. None of them looked Aborigine.

"Those real boomerangs, young fella?" the old geezer asked.

"Yes, sir," Cheekyfella said, his eyes still on the gate. St Cuthbert's was his only connection with Schoolteacher Benson and he didn't want to miss him.

"Is it true those things come back to you when you throw them?" asked the old geezer.

"Sure is, mate," Cheekyfella said.

"Go on, show me!" the old geezer said.

Cheekyfella took one of the boomerangs and spun it high into the air. St Cuthbert's was set back off the road to one side of the bridge across the Bedchester River, so there was no danger of breaking any windows. The weapon went round in a graceful arc and curved back to land in Cheekyfella's hand.

"Wow! Did you see that!" the old geezer

exclaimed admiringly.

A well-dressed man appeared out of nowhere and tossed a 20p coin at Cheekyfella's feet. "Most impressive," he said.

A middle-aged woman stopped. "I missed it," she said. "Can you do it again?"

Cheekyfella threw the boomerang again and caught it coming back. "Very good!" said the woman, smiling. She dropped a 10p coin at Cheekyfella's feet.

A small boy tugged at her dress. "Get him to do it again, Mum," he urged loudly. "Go on, Mum, get him to do it again!"

The mother looked apologetically at Cheekyfella, who smiled and threw the boomerang again. By the time it came back, a small crowd had gathered and there was more money at his feet.

"Have another go!" somebody urged from the back. There was a patter of applause and further coins fell on the pavement.

Cheekyfella sighed and did the trick again. Then, because he discovered he liked applause, he started to show off by throwing both boomerangs at once.

By this stage the trickle through St Cuthbert's gates had become a stream. In the middle of the crowd of pupils he suddenly saw the tall, thin form of Schoolteacher Benson pushing a bicycle. Cheekyfella caught the boomerangs expertly, pushed his way through the growing crowd and started to trot across the road.

"Hey, what about this money?" shouted the old geezer, pointing to all the coins now scattered on the ground.

"You keep it!" Cheekyfella called back. He still had money of his own from selling the first boomerang. He joined the swell of pupils pushing through the gate.

Once inside the school grounds, Cheekyfella left the winding drive and slipped into the bushes. From this vantage point he watched Schoolteacher Benson park his bicycle and disappear into one of the buildings carrying the didgeridoo. Cheekyfella felt a surge of satisfaction. It looked like it was going to be easier than hunting lizards.

A school bell rang and the pupils began to hurry inside. He waited until the drive emptied then emerged from the bushes and trotted up towards the buildings. There was a coach that looked familiar in the main car park and as he got closer, he noticed *INTERNATIONAL STUDENT EXCHANGE PROGRAMME* on the side.

But he was too busy planning his next move to pay much real attention.

It seemed to Cheekyfella what he had to do was clear enough. Now he'd found Schoolteacher Benson, he had to find where Schoolteacher Benson had stashed the sacred didgi and take it back. He might have problems actually getting it home to Oz, but he'd worry about those when the time came.

He slipped back into the bushes, opened his tucker bag and started to turn his face dead white using the paints Scratch gave him. He didn't think he'd find the sacred didgi right away, but he wanted to be ready just in case.

When he was finished, he trotted over to the school building and began, one by one, to look into the windows. He peered into the right classroom just in time to see Schoolteacher Benson putting the sacred didgeridoo away in a cupboard.

Chapter Sixteen

Emma Preston bothered God a lot, so it wasn't surprising she should pray for guidance. She did so in the girls' cloakroom, locked away in one of the loos where she wouldn't be disturbed.

"Hello God," she prayed quietly, but pronouncing each word clearly so God didn't have to strain, "This is Emma here – you may remember I was talking to you last night. Well, I'm sure you've taken care of last night's stuff, but now I'm worried about Mr Benson." A thought struck her and she added, "I'm sorry to be talking to you from a girls' loo – it's the only bit of privacy I get."

She waited in case God should comment. When He didn't, she went on, "The thing is, God, Mr Benson took a didgeridoo from some poor native people in Australia. Mr Benson says it wasn't stealing and I'm sure you will make up your own mind about that – it's certainly not my place to say anything. But the thing is, God, the didgeridoo was guarded by a ghost."

Something struck her and she stopped praying for a moment. She sat looking upwards with a thoughtful frown. Eventually she said, "I'm sorry for the break in transmission, God. I was just wondering if you believed in ghosts. I expect you do since our vicar is always talking about the Holy Ghost. Anyway, whether you believe in them or not, *I* certainly do and besides which I saw one this morning looking through the window."

She stopped again. It was very important to be completely truthful when you were talking to God, so she said, "At least I think it was a ghost. It had a white face and it looked really awful and scary and it stared really hard at Mr Benson, so I'm sure it had something to do with the didgeridoo he sto— he took from the poor native people in Australia."

It occurred to her that she was beginning to waffle, something she did quite often when she got talking to God, so she made an enormous effort to come to the point.

"Anyway, the thing is I don't want Mr Benson to get into any trouble even though I don't like him very much and since I'm the only one who saw the ghost, I thought I'd better try to do something to help. Only I don't know what."

She waited.

God said nothing.

"So I was hoping you might tell me," Emma prompted.

At this point, two of the senior girls clattered into the girls' cloakroom in the middle of a conversation.

"But that's nothing short of *stealing*!" one of them was saying heatedly.

"*She* doesn't think so," said the other.

Emma recognized the voices. She was listening to the St Cuthbert's Head Girl, Kim Beth Poplak, and the senior Hockey Captain, Sheila Slane.

"Well, no," Kim Beth said huffily, "she wouldn't, would she? I mean, as far as she's concerned, any boy she fancies is just there for the taking!"

Emma realized what they were talking about. School gossip had it that Kim Beth's boyfriend had just switched his affections to a bimbo called Belinda. It was fairly obvious from the conversation that Kim Beth didn't like it.

"So what are you going to do?" asked Sheila Slane.

There was the sound of running water. Locked in her cubicle, Emma suddenly began to suspect there was more to the conversation than met the ear. She knew from past experience that God very seldom talked to people in a deep voice out of a cloud these days. Most of the time when He talked to *her* it wasn't a voice at all, more like thoughts coming into her head.

But sometimes He sent messages through other people, arranging for them to say things or do things that had a special meaning.

Emma thought about the conversation between Kim Beth and Sheila. *Nothing short of stealing*, Kim Beth had said. Of course she was talking about Belinda, but perhaps God had arranged for Kim Beth to say that just at the right time for Emma to overhear.

In which case, the conversation wasn't about Kim Beth's boyfriend at all. It was really about Mr Benson.

Nothing short of stealing. Well, God had

made up his mind about *that* all right. And quite properly in Emma's opinion. Taking the sacred didgeridoo from the poor native people of Australia *was* nothing short of stealing. But what was Emma supposed to do about it?

"What are you going to do about it?" Sheila Slane repeated.

Emma froze and placed her ear to the loo door so she wouldn't miss a word. Fortunately the sound of running water stopped.

"I'm going to get him back," Kim Beth said firmly. "I'm going to get him back where he belongs!"

Emma heard the rattle of a locker door, then the cloakroom door, then silence. She waited a moment before letting herself out of the cubicle, then strode from the empty cloakroom with a small, grim smile on her face.

Now she knew what she had to do.

Chapter Seventeen

Emma waited through the last class of the afternoon as Mr Benson droned on about fractions. Her only worry was that when he finished for the day he might take the didgeridoo home with him. But when the final bell rang, he packed his briefcase without going near the cupboard.

He hesitated at the door. "Come along, Emma," he said sharply. "Don't dawdle."

Emma, who was the only one left in the classroom now, dropped to her knees and began searching for an imaginary pencil. "Just getting something I dropped, Mr

Benson," she called cheerfully.

Mr Benson sighed as if the weight of the world's worries was on his shoulders. "Dawdle," he said tiredly, "dawdle, dawdle, dawdle."

For one horrible moment she thought he was going to wait for her, but he only tossed his head dramatically and, still muttering *dawdle*, strode out of the door.

Emma was alone in the empty classroom.

She felt a sudden surge of nervousness, but fought it down. She went over to the classroom door and pushed it closed. Then she looked at the cupboard behind Mr Benson's desk and licked her lips. She wasn't sure what she was going to say if somebody caught her taking the didgeridoo, but she was quite sure she was going to take it.

She wasn't sure how she was going to get it back to the poor natives in Australia either, but she expected God would send her a message about that as well. She thought it was rather nice having God on her side. It made things lovely and easy.

Emma slipped behind Mr Benson's desk and tugged at the cupboard door. It was locked.

Emma glared. When the door still failed to open, she thought for a moment instead. Then she turned to Mr Benson's desk and pulled open one of the drawers.

Her nervousness increased. It was one thing taking the sacred didgeridoo from the cupboard. Pupils were allowed into the cupboard, at least during classtime, to collect new jotters and she was absolutely certain it was right and proper for her to try to return the sacred didgeridoo to its rightful owners.

But rummaging about in Mr Benson's desk was quite another matter. *Nobody* was allowed to do that except Mr Benson.

The drawer she'd opened contained a half-eaten jam sandwich and a ruler. She pulled open another. It was stuffed with papers. A third was empty.

She found a key in the fourth drawer and tried it in the cupboard lock. To her immense relief, it turned easily.

The didgeridoo looked bigger than it had when Mr Benson was waving it about. A *lot* bigger. Emma took it out and stared at it. It was easily light enough to carry, but it was nearly as tall as she was.

Emma found her heart had begun to beat loudly. She wondered why she hadn't thought about this problem before. Taking the didgeridoo from the cupboard was the easy bit, even though the cupboard had been locked.

The hard bit was going to be getting the enormous thing out of the classroom and out of the school.

Hiding it until she worked out how to return it to the poor natives in Australia wasn't going to be all that easy either.

Emma licked lips that had suddenly gone dry. If she was caught trying to take the didgeridoo out of the school she would be in really big trouble. She would certainly be accused of stealing. She might even be *expelled*.

For a moment she actually considered putting the wretched thing back in the cupboard and leaving it there. But then she remembered God was on her side.

Emma went to the classroom door, opened it a crack and peered through. The corridor was empty. She hefted the sacred didgeridoo like a long, fat spear, took a deep breath, uttered a small prayer and slipped outside.

Chapter Eighteen

Cheekyfella ducked down below the level of the window. He didn't think Schoolteacher Benson had spotted him, but one of the pupils, a pretty fair-haired girl with plaits, had looked directly at him and turned a little pale.

He crouched, waiting, his senses on maximum alert. But if she was raising the alarm, nobody was paying any attention. The only sound he could hear was Schoolteacher Benson droning on.

After a while, Cheekyfella ran quickly across the open space and slipped back into the bushes.

It seemed to him that the simplest plan was best. He would wait in the bushes until school finished and watch for Schoolteacher Benson coming out.

If Schoolteacher Benson was carrying the didgi, Cheekyfella would stalk him like a boomer until they reached his home. Then he'd wait until Schoolteacher Benson left the didgi down somewhere, slip in and take it back.

All easy for a hunter.

If Schoolteacher Benson left St Cuthbert's without the didgi, it would be even simpler. Cheekyfella would slip in and take it from the cupboard.

So Cheekyfella squatted in the middle of the bush, thankful for the concealment, and settled down to wait.

Around midday, Schoolteacher Benson came out (without the didgi) as did most of the pupils. Cheekyfella reckoned it must be lunch-time.

He was tempted to nick in and take the didgi there and then, but lunch-time or not, there were still too many people around for him to risk it.

He settled back to wait some more. Since his stomach had begun to growl and there was nothing left in his tucker bag, he dug idly in the soft earth at the base of the bush until he found some worms and ate them. They didn't have the nutty flavour of witchetty grubs, but they took the edge off his hunger.

He didn't feel thirsty at all. He hadn't felt thirsty since he came to Pomland, even though he'd noticed that the Poms drank vast quantities of tea. He wondered if it might be addictive.

As he waited, he thought about living in Pomland and decided he much preferred his native Oz. Apart from the fact that the grubs tasted better, he still found the Pomland weather far too cold and wet, even in bright sunshine.

He didn't like the lifestyle either. Even the short time he'd been here was enough for him to notice the overcrowding, the endless traffic and the fact that Poms never smiled at strangers.

What made it even worse was that young Poms were herded into schools, just like white kids in Oz. None of them ever seemed to learn anything sensible from their parents and the stuff they learned from their teachers at places like St Cuthbert's was pretty weird – the history of countries that were none of their business and how to count more things than anybody would ever see.

There was nothing about hunting or how to find water underground or which plants were good for healing, or anything at all useful.

The interval between classes was marked by short bursts on the school bell. The end of the school day was marked by a much longer burst.

Cheekyfella watched the pupils swarm from the building, laughing, shouting, jostling one another. It looked as if they didn't really like school. In fact they were all so eager to get home that the school grounds were almost deserted before Schoolteacher Benson appeared. He was carrying his briefcase, but no didgi.

Cheekyfella smiled to himself. The whole thing had been so easy. A little walk in the outback. A little trip to Pomland. A little walk in the wet. And now the sacred didgi was within his grasp.

He waited until the place was completely empty before he came out of his bush. He had a minute of confusion after he stepped into the school, but his hunter's instinct came to his aid and he soon found the classroom he'd seen through the window.

The cupboard behind the desk had a key sticking out of it, but it wasn't locked.

Cheekyfella pulled it open with a grunt of triumph.

The sacred didgi wasn't there.

Chapter Nineteen

Emma Preston woke early, feeling nervous. After a while she remembered why. The sacred didgeridoo of the Aranda Tribe was hidden under her bed and she had absolutely no idea how to get it back to its rightful owners.

In fact, she was having serious doubts about taking it in the first place, even if God had gone to all the trouble of sending her a message. If she was caught with the silly thing now, she'd be branded a thief, the didgi would be taken away and its real owners would never see it again.

The trouble with God, she thought, was that He only ever told you what He wanted you to do. He never bothered telling you how to do it.

She dragged herself out of bed, took a quick shower, pulled on her school uniform and went downstairs to the usual chaos created by her mother.

This morning it was greater chaos than usual.

"Got to hurry!" her mother shouted, rushing here and there. "Lots to organize! Lots to do! Must get a move on! No time to waste! Everything must go chop-chop!" She was wearing her tweed suit. Her rolled umbrella stood near the door. Mungo, the terrier, raced after her excitedly.

Emma's father, who was well used to mornings by now, sat by the window nibbling a piece of toast. He was a man just as thin as Schoolteacher Benson, but with far kinder features. His hair was completely white. Emma expected that was from living with her mother.

"Morning, Daddy," Emma said as she sat down and reached for the Corn Flakes.

Her father looked up from his toast and regarded her vaguely for a moment. She often wondered if he really knew who she was at this time of the morning. But his face creased into a smile and he said cheerfully, "Good morning, Emma." He was always cheerful, always calm. Emma's mother said it came from being a museum curator. It was a job that allowed him to live in the past.

"Do you have a busy day today, Daddy?" Emma asked politely.

He beamed at her benignly. "Not really, darling. Just the 1866 Sheep Stealing Treaty to frame." He glanced at his toast then at the rushing figure of his wife. "Bit of a flap on, I'm afraid." He tapped the side of his nose significantly. "Her exchange students, you know."

Emma knew all right. Her mother's passion was the Student Exchange Scheme. She spent her life rushing from one part of the country to another, ferrying students about in coaches.

On the rare times she was at home, most of her time was spent *planning* to race from one part of the country to another, ferrying students about in coaches.

The latest batch of exchange students had arrived at St Cuthbert's only a few days ago, but her mother's behaviour suggested they were moving on already. She asked her father.

"That's right," he nodded benignly. "They must be quite dizzy by now, poor things." He smiled again. "At least she's not going with them to the airport – just seeing them off at the school – so they'll have a chance to rest on the coach."

Emma poured milk on her Corn Flakes, but decided against adding extra sugar.

"Where do they go next?" she asked. Exchange students went all over the world, part of a lunatic plan to promote international understanding.

Her father was staring out the window at the antics of a sparrow. He dragged his attention back with difficulty. "I think Australia," he said vaguely.

Emma froze with a spoonful of Corn Flakes half way to her mouth. She'd just had a second message from God.

Now she knew how to get the sacred didgeridoo back home.

Chapter Twenty

Cheekyfella Tabagee turned up at St Cuthbert's very early next morning and secreted himself in the centre of the bush that was now starting to feel like home.

He had spent an uncomfortable night under the bridge – too cold, too damp and too much traffic overhead – but at least it had given him time to think.

When the first rush of panic died down, he consoled himself with the idea that the missing didgi probably wouldn't stay missing for long. Even though Schoolteacher Benson definitely hadn't taken it home with him, the fact that it wasn't in the cupboard more than likely only meant he'd moved it before going home.

All Cheekyfella had to do was wait. Sooner or later, Schoolteacher Benson was bound to go to wherever he'd put it. Once Cheekyfella knew where the didgi was, he had only to be patient and wait his chance. And Cheekyfella knew he had a lot of patience.

He'd finally gone to sleep with the plan all worked out. And even in the morning it looked like a good plan.

He waited to see how it would pan out.

Schoolteacher Benson came to school and went into his classroom just before the bell, more or less as Cheekyfella had expected. But after that, the plan began to fall apart.

First off, when the bell sounded, the school grounds didn't clear the way they should. Dozens of students hung around outside instead of rushing into the buildings to join their classes.

Cheekyfella was still trying to figure out why when the coach with *INTERNATIONAL STUDENT EXCHANGE PROGRAMME* on the side came rumbling slowly into the main courtyard. At much the same time, a familiar figure in a tweed suit appeared out of nowhere, wielding her umbrella and shouting orders. Her small dog was yapping at her heels.

Cheekyfella watched curiously and might have waited until everybody left if it hadn't been for that yappy dog. The little brute, which still looked skinny as a half dead dingo and twice as ugly, suddenly picked up a scent.

It raced around for half a minute, nose pressed to the tarmac, then suddenly headed in Cheekyfella's direction, barking furiously.

"Go away! Shoo!" hissed Cheekyfella from his hiding place.

The dog glared in at him maliciously, hackles raised. The barking continued without pause.

For a moment, Cheekyfella considered trying to stun it with his boomerang, but reluctantly decided against it. His pa, Joe Tabagee, had always taught him never to use the boomerang on an animal unless he planned to eat it. Just the thought of eating this yapping little monster gave him indigestion.

All the same, he had to do something. He felt no fear of the little dog, but sooner or later the barking was going to draw attention to his hiding place. Once anybody came to investigate, he was discovered for sure.

He thought about it for a minute then remembered something Scratching Woman told him years before. Sometimes the best place to hide is under people's noses. The swirling crowd of students included some black faces. Since he wasn't expecting to find the didgi right away, he hadn't painted his that morning, so he looked just as black as the others. He reckoned if he could slip amongst them, nobody would notice in all the confusion.

Cheekyfella did just that. The dog followed him yapping, but backed off to avoid getting trampled as Cheekyfella slipped into the crowd.

And that was when everything suddenly went wrong.

The woman in the tweed suit snapped an order. The crowd surged forward, carrying Cheekyfella with it. In seconds, Cheekyfella realized to his horror everybody was heading for the coach.

Without hesitation, he fought his way free and started off down the drive. He hoped nobody would notice, but even so, discovery was preferable to being shunted on to the coach.

Somebody did notice. The end of Mrs Preston's umbrella hooked into the back of his T-shirt. "Oh, no, you don't, young man!" she said. "You're the boy who slipped away at the airport – I'm certainly not letting you do that again!"

The little dog raced down to snap irritatingly at his heels as the woman in the tweed suit overrode his protests and bundled him on to the coach.

"Off you go!" she ordered the driver briskly.

"But Missus –" shouted Cheekyfella.

Everybody ignored him. The coach doors hissed shut. The engine roared into life and, to his horror, they started moving.

Chapter Twenty-One

Emma emerged from under the seat as soon as she judged she was well out of sight of her mother.

She knew both her parents would be very cross, but she'd left them a letter explaining everything and telling them not to worry. She knew deep in her heart she was doing the right thing.

"Hi, Emma," said one of the exchange students, a look of surprise on her face. "I didn't know you were coming with us."

"Last minute decision," Emma told her shortly.

She had a small worry that her disappearance might be noticed before she was safely on the plane. But it was only small. Her father would be at the museum all day. Her mother *might* just return to the house, but it was unlikely. Having seen off one batch of exchange students, she would almost certainly head straight for her little office to organize the next.

Mr Benson might notice she was not in class, or he might not. But even if he did, he'd only think she was off sick.

She sank back into the coach seat and looked out the window. The English countryside flashed by. The sacred didgeridoo was in the rack above her head. She'd wrapped it in brown paper and tied it with string, so it looked like a peculiar parcel. Apart from an overnight bag, it was the only luggage she was carrying.

There was a bad moment when she reached the airport. Emma had been hoping against hope that nothing would draw attention to her, but as the group filed through the security check, a uniformed official stopped her.

"What's in the package, Miss?" he asked politely enough, but without a hint of a smile.

"Nothing," Emma said instinctively. The rest of the coach group had gone through and were waiting for her by the departure gates.

The man leaned over his little counter for a closer look. "Has the appearance of something nasty," he told her seriously.

"It isn't," Emma said. She felt a little flowering of panic.

"Looks like a rifle," said the man. "Or maybe a bazooka."

Emma wondered what sort of idiot would imagine an eleven-year-old girl might be carrying a bazooka. Then it occurred to her she had no need to hide what was in the package. Mr Benson was miles away. Her mother was miles away. Nobody on the coach would have any idea that the didgeridoo wasn't hers.

She felt the panic drain away to such an extent that she actually smiled. "It's not a bazooka – it's a didgeridoo."

He blinked. "What?"

"It's a didgeridoo," Emma repeated. "I'm taking it to Australia."

"Pull the other one," the man scowled. "Nobody takes didgeridoos to Australia. That's where they come from."

"But it is a didgeridoo – honestly!" Emma protested. She was aware a restless queue was building up behind her.

The official looked at Emma, looked at the package, then looked back at Emma again. "I think I'd better see it for myself," he said.

Emma quickly unwrapped the brown paper from the didgeridoo. The official stared at it in amazement. "Good grief," he said, "it really is a didgeridoo!"

"Can I go now?" Emma asked.

Still shaking his head in amazement, the airport official waved her through.

As she began to wrap up the instrument again, Emma glanced back to smile apologetically at the waiting crowd.

To her horror, the ghost she'd seen peering through the window of the classroom was no more than fifty feet away, glaring at her malevolently. It was so enraged, its face had turned from white to black.

Chapter Twenty-Two

Cheekyfella stared in amazement. Once he left the coach he'd been trying to slip away when he saw the sacred didgi. It was wrapped in brown paper, but he'd know the shape anywhere.

At first he couldn't believe it. He'd been so certain the didgi was somewhere at St Cuthbert's that he'd spent the whole coach trip figuring out ways of getting back there.

Now the didgi had turned up at the airport – carried by an exchange student sheila with Schoolteacher Benson nowhere in sight! It was weird. He wondered if Scratch's spirit had anything to do with it.

For a moment, Cheekyfella just stood there, his jaw hanging. Then the sheila turned and looked right at him.

At once she went pale. At once she turned and hurried, almost running, towards the departure gates. Cheekyfella blinked. He didn't think he looked *that* ugly.

Then he caught himself and started to run after her. However the didgi got here, the girl had it now, so he mustn't lose her.

It was easier said than done.

"Here, where do you think you're going?" shouted the security guard as Cheekyfella tried to push past the queue.

"I'm with them!" lied Cheekyfella, pointing at the group of exchange students filing through the departure gates. The sheila with the sacred didgi filed through with them.

"What's that you're taking through?" the guard asked suspiciously.

"Just two boomerangs and a tucker-bag," Cheekyfella told him.

"You're taking *boomerangs* to Australia?" asked the guard. "What's going on here? I've just had a kid through carrying a didgeridoo!"

"It must be these underground bomb tests," a man in the queue suggested. "It's starting to affect their brains."

"Sir —" said Cheekyfella desperately. Out of the corner of his eye, he could see the last of the coach group disappearing through the departure gate.

"Better let me have a look," the guard said.

Cheekyfella pushed the boomerangs and the tucker-bag at him in a panic of impatience. He half thought of making a run for it, but decided that would solve nothing.

The official held up the boomerangs in amazement. "Good grief," he said, "these really *are* boomerangs!"

"Sir –" said Cheekyfella again, dancing on one foot and casting frantic glances towards the departure gate.

But the man was opening the tucker bag. He peered inside short-sightedly. "What are these?" he asked. "They look like worms."

"They *are* worms," Cheekyfella told him. He could hardly wait to get back to his witchetty grubs, but at least worms were easy to find in Pomland and they kept him going even if they didn't taste as good.

"Oh well now," the guard said, drawing himself up to his full height. "You can't take these through. It's against agricultural export regulations."

"You keep them, sir!" cried Cheekyfella. "Keep them all! Keep the tucker-bag!" All he wanted was to get away before the sacred didgi disappeared for ever.

But the guard was shaking his head. "Can't do that," he said. "Worms aren't my department. You'll have to turn them in at the Agricultural Exports Office and fill in a form in triplicate."

"I haven't time for that!" screamed Cheekyfella.

"Can't take them with you. Can't leave them here," the guard insisted.

Cheekyfella grabbed the tucker-bag and stuffed the worms into his mouth. He chewed and swallowed. "There!" he said. "Can I go through now?"

The guard turned pale, his eyes rolled upwards and he sank slowly to the floor.

Cheekyfella snatched the boomerangs and ran towards the departure gate. It closed as he reached it.

"Sorry, son," a uniformed attendant said. "Australian plane's just taking off. I'm afraid you've missed it."

Chapter Twenty-Three

By the time the plane took off, Emma was in the middle of a heavy worry.

She'd made it on board as part of the student exchange party. She was being looked after by smiling air hostesses as part of the student exchange party. Nobody had asked a single awkward question.

But she wasn't part of the student exchange party and sooner or later somebody was going to find that out.

She reckoned the most likely time for that to happen was when they landed in Australia. That's when passports would be handed in, documents would be checked, heads counted.

Her chances of getting through would be zero.

On top of all this, it now looked as if she was being chased by the didgeridoo ghost.

Although it should by rights have been haunting Mr Benson, it probably didn't realize she was trying to bring the sacred didgeridoo back, so it was after her now.

Emma worried until the NO SMOKING FASTEN SEAT BELTS sign went off, then got up and headed for the loo.

"Hello, God," she said softly after she had locked the door. "I'm sorry to keep calling you from loos, but I'm in a bit of bother and I don't want to draw attention to myself."

She stopped. It occurred to her that God might not recognize her since she was praying from 30,000 feet. So she said carefully, "This is Emma here, God. You know – the one who asked you about the sacred didgeridoo."

Then, since a little flattery never did any harm, she added, "It was ever so clever of you to send me a message the way you did and I've done what you told me."

She stopped again, half hoping for a whisper of encouragement. When none came, she went on:

"The thing is, God, I've got the didgeridoo all right, but I'm not sure they'll let me into Australia to give it back. I mean, I don't have a passport or anything. So maybe you could let me know what I should do next. And please don't tell me God helps those who help themselves. I've been helping myself for ages now so I'm not passing the buck or anything. It's just that I could really do with a bit of help."

As an afterthought she added, "You know I mentioned about the ghost, God? Well, it's after me now. I saw it at the airport and it isn't even white now – it's gone black with rage. Anyway, I thought you might like to tell it to leave me alone. I know it's a ghost, but you're God, so it has to do what you say. Thanks a million. I really would appreciate that."

Because she was on a plane, she concluded, "Roger, wilco, over and out, God."

She waited for a reply.

It occurred to her that since she was now in the clouds herself, a deep voice was not entirely out of the question, but none came.

She waited for a voice in her head, or even a thought that didn't seem to be hers, but there was nothing of this sort either.

She waited for a sudden burst of inspiration. Nothing.

She was right on the point of giving up when someone hammered on the toilet door.

"Are you planning to stay in there all day?" an angry voice demanded.

Emma got the point at once. "Thank you, God," she whispered.

Chapter Twenty-Four

Cheekyfella walked up to a tall fat man with palm trees on his shirt.

"Excuse me, Yankee sir," he said politely, "but would you like to buy a boomerang?"

He held up one of his two remaining weapons.

The big man peered at it rheumily. His breath smelled of Bushmills whisky. "Let's have a look," he said.

Cheekyfella handed over a boomerang. The big man turned it over in his hands, examining the carvings. "This genuine Australian Abbo?" he asked.

"Fair dinkum," Cheekyfella confirmed.

Without warning, the big man hurled the boomerang into the air. It sailed above the crowded airport concourse and smashed an illuminated advertising hoarding for Winston's cigarettes.

The big man stared up at it, swaying a little. "Didn't come back," he said disconsolately and walked away.

Cheekyfella retrieved the boomerang. As he was brushing it free of broken glass, a plump lady pushing a tea trolley stopped beside him.

"'Ere," she said, "is that one of them boomerang things wot they have in Horstralia?"

"Yes, Ma'am," Cheekyfella said. He looked around for more palm trees.

"Wouldn't think of selling, would you?" the plump lady asked.

Cheekyfella blinked and looked at her properly for the first time.

"Only my boy Billy is mad keen about anything Horstralian," the woman said before he could reply. "And it's his birfday coming up and I thought it would be nice to get him somefing genuine from Down Under, if you catch my meaning." She peered at Cheekyfella expectantly.

"Yes," Cheekyfella replied. "Yes, please."

"Yes wot?"

"Yes, I would think of selling," Cheekyfella said. He glanced at the debris of the Winston's sign. "It really does come back," he added. "The big fella just threw it wrong."

"If you say so, I'm sure." The woman took the boomerang gently from Cheekyfella's hand and stroked it lovingly. "My Billy would love this. How much do you want for it?"

Cheekyfella took a deep breath. "Nine hundred and fifty five pounds," he said.

The plump lady continued to examine the

boomerang. "Bit steep for a boomerang," she remarked. "Even if it does come back."

Cheekyfella thought so too, but nine hundred and fifty five pounds was what the ticket man had told him was the cost of a one-way flight back to Australia and he didn't know how else he was going to raise the money.

He thought he'd better explain. He didn't want the nice plump lady to think he was a rip-off merchant.

She listened without comment until he'd finished. "So it's not that you *really* want nine hundred and fifty five pounds," she said thoughtfully. "It's just that you want to get back home."

"But getting home will cost nine hundred and fifty five pounds," Cheekyfella said.

"Not necessarily," the woman said. "You come with me."

She led him across the concourse, expertly carving a passage with her trolley. Two uniformed security men raced by in the direction of the broken sign. Neither gave Cheekyfella a second glance. Cheekyfella and the woman reached a door marked *Strictly Private*. To his surprise, she walked straight in.

Cheekyfella followed her, then stopped. They were in as plush a lounge as he had ever seen. It was full of uniformed airline personnel.

"Come on," the plump lady said. She left her trolley by the door, took him by the hand and led him up to a tall, distinguished man with SENIOR PILOT on his cap. He turned round at her approach and smiled broadly. "Hello, Mum," he said.

"Hello, Billy," said the plump lady. "I got somebody here wants to meet you."

Chapter Twenty-Five

Emma waited until she was certain all the air hostesses were looking the other way, then nipped back to the loo. She saw the NO SMOKING FASTEN SEAT BELTS sign light up just as she closed the door.

She settled down to wait.

Emma crouched in the loo as the plane touched down, crouched as it taxied to a halt. She was still crouching when the passengers got off in a buzz of excited conversation.

It was important, she thought, to make sure the coast was completely clear, so she stayed where she was for a full half hour.

By that time, all sounds of movement in the plane had ceased. She opened the door a crack and peered out. There was no one in sight. The body of the plane was empty.

Emma stepped out of the loo. The plane shook suddenly, then began to move. Emma dived back into the loo and clung to the wash basin for dear life. She'd left it too long. The plane was going to take off again.

But after a few moments, the plane stopped moving. This time Emma shot from the loo and peered through a window.

What she saw was reassuring. The plane now stood beside a red brick building in a near-deserted area of the airport. Fat fuel lines snaked across the ground. Mechanics in overalls strolled lazily around. Nobody was paying any attention at all to the aircraft. She reckoned if she picked her time just right, she could slip away without anybody ever noticing.

The problem was she couldn't leave the plane.

The main exit door was closed and even when she found the controls to open it, she found she was high above the ground – far too high to jump.

She closed the door before anyone noticed and went back inside to think.

After a while it occurred to her that the pilot wasn't likely to leave the plane the same way as the passengers. There was probably some sort of folding stairway from the cockpit.

She made her way to the front of the plane, but found access to the cockpit blocked by a locked door.

She went back and sat in a seat. She started wondering about luggage. She'd taken her bag and the didgeridoo in with her because they were small, but large luggage, she knew, was loaded on somewhere else. Which meant it was taken off somewhere else.

The only trouble was she had no idea *where* it was taken off, or how she could get there.

She was wondering if she should have another word with God when out of nowhere she remembered a TV movie she'd seen about a plane crash. All the passengers had got out by means of an emergency chute.

Emma started to search the plane. Twenty minutes later she struck gold. The notice, above a large red button, said:

```
ESCAPE CHUTE
EMERGENCY USE ONLY
```

Emma took a last look through the window and saw to her delight even the mechanics seemed to have disappeared. She collected the sacred didgeridoo and her overnight bag from the luggage rack, then firmly pressed the button.

There was a hiss of compressed air and a sloping canvas passageway opened up miraculously in front of her. She dropped the bag and didgeridoo into it and watched them disappear. Then she sat down on her bottom, let go of the sides and slid.

Moments later she was on the ground.

She glanced around. Her luck was still holding – there was nobody about. She picked up the didgeridoo and the bag and started off around the corner of the red brick building.

As she did so, a hand fell on her shoulder.

Chapter Twenty-Six

Cheekyfella sat in the cockpit of the 747 goggle-eyed. Everywhere he looked there were dials and gauges, red lights, green lights, flickering needles and heaven knew what else.

"How do you learn what all that stuff *means*?" he asked.

Captain Billy shrugged. "A crate this size mainly flies herself," he said. "We watch her on take-off and landing, but in between she's pretty much on auto."

Up ahead through the window there was a white wool carpet of clouds. It looked so solid

Cheekyfella felt he could step outside and walk on it. He knew Scratching Woman and the other Clever Men sometimes left their bodies to fly around like birds and wondered if they ever got to 30,000 feet. The scenery up here was something else. He'd missed it on the trip out on account of travelling in a crate.

"Sandwich?" Captain Billy asked, passing him a plastic lunch box. "We've a long way to go and Mum says I have to look after you."

They were crossing the Australian coastline many hours later before Cheekyfella asked the question on his mind.

"You know the boomerang I let your mum have for your birthday, Billy?"

"It's a corker, Cheekyfella!" Billy said enthusiastically. "Thank you so much."

"I was wondering," Cheekyfella said, "you being a pilot and all, going to Australia anyway, how come you didn't buy one for yourself?"

Captain Billy grinned ruefully. "I became

a pilot because I wanted to see the world. But all I get to see is foreign airports. No time for anything else." He glanced at his co-pilot. "Right, Sam?"

"Right, Billy," Sam said sourly.

Billy shrugged. "I've been to Australia fifteen times, New York more than that, Bahrain, Rome, Paris, Moscow, Copenhagen, Cairo, Athens, you name it. But the only *country* I ever get to see is dear old Britain."

Watching the plane landing was a thrill a minute. An air hostess sheila called Sheila chatted to him because Billy and Sam were too busy once the auto-pilot was switched off. By the time they taxied down the runway, Cheekyfella had decided if ever he left the Outback he was going to train as a pilot. He didn't care about seeing other countries. What he wanted was to fly planes.

"Keep your head down," Billy warned him as they rolled to a full stop. "You're not supposed to have left Oz in the first place, so we're going to have to sneak you back in."

"Just get me off the plane," Cheekyfella said confidently. "I reckon I can take it from there."

"Reckon you could at that," Sam said admiringly.

But getting back into Oz was the least of Cheekyfella's problems. What he had to do before anything was find the girl with the sacred didgi. He put the problem to Billy.

"She must have taken the Qantas flight that took off before us," Billy mused thoughtfully. "That crate would have touched down about half an hour ago. They'll hold her until tomorrow, give her a service then send her out again. I could show you where she's parked if that's any help?"

Cheekyfella doubted it. The girl could be anywhere in half an hour. At the same time he had to start looking somewhere and you never knew what a hunter might pick up.

"Thanks, Billy. Much appreciated."

It turned out he was glad he took the offer. As he approached the Qantas plane, Cheekyfella was amazed to see the girl heading for a large red brick building. He sprinted quietly to catch her up and placed a hand upon her shoulder.

Chapter Twenty-Seven

Emma jumped back in alarm. She'd been caught by the ghost.

"Keep away from me!" she gasped.

"You've got our didgi," Cheekyfella said.

Emma fingered a small crucifix hanging round her neck, then suddenly held it up in the manner of someone warding off a vampire. "Get back!" she said desperately. "You don't have to haunt me any more."

Cheekyfella blinked. "What's this haunting business?"

Emma peered at the boy before her. Close up, he didn't look much like a ghost.

She reached out cautiously and poked him in the arm. He was completely solid and quite warm.

"You're not a ghost," she said.

"Not yet," Cheekyfella told her. He decided ghosts were a red herring and got back to the main point. "You've got our didgi," he repeated. "It's the sacred didgi of the Aranda people."

"I know," said Emma shortly. "I was bringing it back."

Cheekyfella blinked again. "You were?"

"Definitely," said Emma. "At least if I can get out of this airport and find my way to the people it belongs to."

Suddenly Cheekyfella grinned. "I think I can help you there," he said.

Chapter Twenty-Eight

It took far longer with the young white Pom sheila Emma than it would have on his own.

She needed far more water than he did and had to rest a lot because of the heat. She was difficult about food as well. She wouldn't eat roots unless he cooked them and she wouldn't eat witchetty grubs at all. At night she insisted he build shelters to keep away spiders and scorpions.

But despite the hassles, Cheekyfella got her to Middle Bone eventually.

The gathering was gone, of course, but

Wally and the Elders were still there, along with the Aranda who lived full time in the Bush.

"Better let me go ahead," said Cheekyfella. "Tell them who you are."

Emma stared out across the wasteland at the scattering of dark figures. Most of them looked half-starved, the rest looked half-mad, but she was well beyond caring. "OK by me," she said. She slid down into the shade of a rock.

"I think I'd better take the didgi," Cheekyfella said.

Emma nodded without speaking. She was sweaty, dirty and exhausted. She liked Cheekyfella a lot now she'd got to know him, but they'd walked what felt like a thousand miles together in this heat. She was beginning to hope that if God had any more little jobs for her, He'd keep them to Himself.

Cheekyfella trotted over to Porcupine

Rock. Wally Arkady was squatting with his back against it.

"G'day, Cheekyfella," Wally said.

"G'day, Wally," Cheekyfella said. It felt good to be back.

"See you got it," Wally said, nodding to the sacred didgi.

"Too right, Wally," Cheekyfella grinned.

"Much trouble?"

"Piece of cake."

Wally glanced beyond him at the figure flaked out in the shade. "Who's the sheila, Cheekyfella?"

"Name of Emma Preston, Wally," Cheekyfella said. "She's *really* the one who got back the didgi."

"Better bring her over," Wally said.

When Cheekyfella trotted back, Emma allowed herself to be led by the hand towards one of the ugliest men she had ever seen in her life. He wore tattered khaki shorts and nothing else.

"This is Wally Arkady, Emma," Cheekyfella told her. "He's chief of our people."

Emma wondered if the chief could speak English, but before she had time to ask, Wally said, "G'day, Emma. Cheekyfella tells me we have you to thank for getting back our didgi."

"I didn't think it fair that my teacher stole it," Emma explained. Close up, Wally Arkady looked even uglier than at a distance, but he had a nice voice.

"Good on you!" Wally said. "You interested in a reward?"

Emma blinked. She hadn't thought of a reward. She glanced at the tribespeople who had started to gather round, eyeing her curiously. Most of them didn't even seem to own clothes.

"What I had in mind," Wally said, as if reading her thoughts, "was making you a blood sister of the Aranda People. That way you can come visit any time without having to worry about passports or any of that nonsense."

"Yes, please!" Emma beamed.

Cheekyfella was beaming too, but there was something else he had to see about. "Hey, Wally," he said. "My pa about? I want to tell him he's about to be made an Elder."

A gloomy expression settled over Wally's features. "He's over at the mining camp, Cheekyfella. Watching to make sure those boys don't start cutting up our song lines a minute before the Law allows them."

"But they can't touch the land now we've got our didgi back!" Cheekyfella protested.

Wally sighed and stood up. He put an arm around Cheekyfella's shoulders. "Didgi only gets our magic back," he said. "We don't get our land unless we can find a copy of the Sheep Stealing Treaty we made with the Poms back in the old days."

"Is that the Sheep Stealing Treaty of

1866?" asked Emma suddenly.

There was a moment of absolute silence. Nobody moved. Nobody spoke. Then Wally said very quietly, "How did you know?"

"My dad's got a copy of it in his museum," said Emma. "He was talking about framing it the day I left."

A slow, slow smile broke over Wally's ugly face. "I think this calls for another Singing. A real big celebration. Emma, you and Cheekyfella can lead the dance."

Glossary

Aborigine   The first inhabitants of Australia. Latest finds show they arrived maybe 70,000 years ago and they're still hanging in, despite all odds, today.

Ancestors   The Ancestors were the first of everything that lives – not just humanity, but animals, birds and insects like kangaroos, wallabies, dingoes, kookaburras, grubs and what have you. When Aborigines talk about, say, the Kookaburra Man, they mean the first spirit ancestor of the kookaburra birds you see today.

Aranda The largest Aborigine tribe in Australia.

Bandicoot A small Australian marsupial that lives on insects and vegetation.

Billabong Stream.

Blackfella European term for Aborigine.

Boomer Kangaroo.

Boomerang Aborigine hunting weapon, some types of which circle round and return to the thrower if they miss their prey.

Carpet snake Native Australia snake.

Clever Man Aborigine shaman or witch-doctor.

Clicksticks Two carved sticks tapped together to beat out a rhythm by the Aborigines.

Corroboree Aborigine term for a gathering.

Didgeridoo Aborigine musical instrument made from a tree branch that has been hollowed out by termites. Aborigines learn a peculiar circular breathing to play it.

Dingo A wild dog native to Australia.

Dreaming Every Aborigine has a Dreaming that links him to a special Ancestor and hence to a particular animal or bird. These Dreamings mean the Aborigines feel themselves part of nature, drawing help and strength from the animals of their particular Dreaming.

Dreamtime The time when the world was made, according to Aborigine myth. But the Dreamtime is also now, in another dimension ...

Humpie A small temporary Aboriginal dwelling, usually thrown together with whatever materials might be found to hand.

Kookaburra A bird native to Australia, sometimes called the Laughing Jackass because of its peculiar call.

Kookaburra Man See Ancestors.

Old Man Kangaroo See Ancestors.

Platypus A dopey-looking marsupial with a beak like a duck and a body like a cuddly otter.

Pom An English person.

Pomland Great Britain.

Qantas Australia's national airline.

Singing Secret Aborigine ceremony, dating back to the Dreamtime, in which members of a tribe will sing the ancient songs that keep their land from reverting back to the primeval chaos.

Song lines   Invisible tracks the Aborigines believe were laid down by their first ancestors so people could find their way through Australia.

Spinifex   A type of Australian grass with spiky leaves and seeds.

Wallaby   A small species of kangaroo.

Whinging Pom   An English person.

Witchetty   A fat white grub eaten alive and wriggling by the Australian Aborigines, who consider it a delicacy.

Woomera   A spear-thrower invented by the Australian Aborigines that allows them to hurl spears further and harder than the usual way.